WHERE'S WALLY?

GAMES ON THE GO!

PUZZLES • ACTIVITIES • SEARCHES

MARTIN HANDFORD

WALKER BOOKS
AND SUBSIDIARIES
LONDON • BOSTON • SYDNEY • AUCKLAND

HI THERE, PUZZLE LOVERS!

JOIN ME – WALLY – AND MY FRIENDS WOOF, WENDA, WIZARD WHITEBEARD AND ODLAW FOR SOME TRICKY TEASERS AND PUZZLING PUZZLES.

THERE ARE ALL SORTS OF CHALLENGES BETWEEN THESE PAGES, AND EVEN A FOLD-OUT BOARD GAME TO PLAY – WOW! YOU CAN TAKE THIS WITH YOU ANYWHERE: IN THE CAR, ON A TRAIN, ON A PLANE, FLYING IN A HOT AIR BALLOON ... EVEN AT HOME ON THE SOFA!

STRETCH YOUR BRAIN TO ITS LIMITS WITH THE MIND-BOGGLING GAMES AND OTHER INCREDIBLE THINGS TO FIND AND DO ALONG THE WAY.

DON'T FORGET TO KEEP AN EYE OUT FOR THE
WALLY-WATCHERS. THEY COULD APPEAR AT ANY TIME!

PLUS PLENTY OF MY OLD PALS ARE WANDERING
BETWEEN THE SCENES, SO STAY ALERT!

SOME SEARCHES AREN'T AS SIMPLE AS THEY
FIRST APPEAR AND SOME CODES ARE MORE CRACKABLE
THAN YOU MIGHT THINK, BUT ALL THE PUZZLES, GAMES
AND BRAIN-BUSTERS ARE GREAT FUN! SO, GO ALONE
OR INVITE SOME FRIENDS TO HELP YOU,
AND LET THE JOURNEY BEGIN!

Wally

HI THERE, WALLY FANS!

I'M OFF ON ANOTHER ADVENTURE, AND YOU CAN COME TOO! BUT WATCH OUT, THERE ARE SOME PERPLEXING, PRACTICALLY IMPOSSIBLE PUZZLES IN THIS POCKET-SIZED COMPENDIUM! WOOF, WIZARD WHITEBEARD, WENDA, ODLAW AND I HAVE COME ACROSS ALL SORTS OF MANIC MAYHEM ON OUR TRAVELS, AND IT'S UP TO YOU TO HELP US OUT. IT'S MY GO FIRST! CAN YOU CRACK THIS SELECTION OF WACKY WORD PUZZLES, SILLY SEARCHES AND OTHER TOPSY-TURVY TRICKS? GOOD LUCK!

Wally

TRAVEL ESSENTIALS

Wally is about to set off on his travels.
Check he's carrying everything from the list
below, and then find the objects he's missing
in the scene behind. Bon voyage!

BALLOON
BELT
KETTLE
FLOWER
CUP
MALLET
TOP HAT
SLEEPING BAG
BUCKET
POMPOM
SATCHEL

WALKING STICK
BINOCULARS
RUCKSACK
CAMERA
SPINNING TOP
SNORKEL
CLOCK
SPADE

MORE THINGS TO DO

There are some things Wally can't
travel with! Unscramble the letters
below to find out what he's leaving
behind!

cirgan rac   *Clue: vroom vroom*
dgrna iapno   *Clue: musical keys*
ckhneti snki   *Clue: wash the dishes*

5

HALL OF MIRRORS

Look closely at each of the mirrors. In one mirror Wally is facing in
the opposite direction – can you spot him?

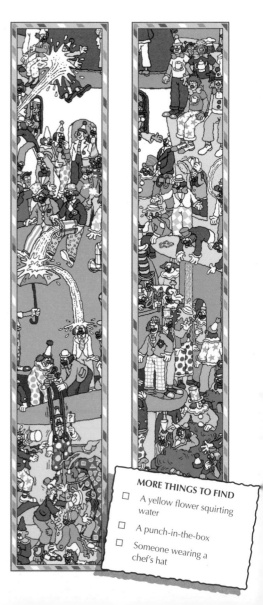

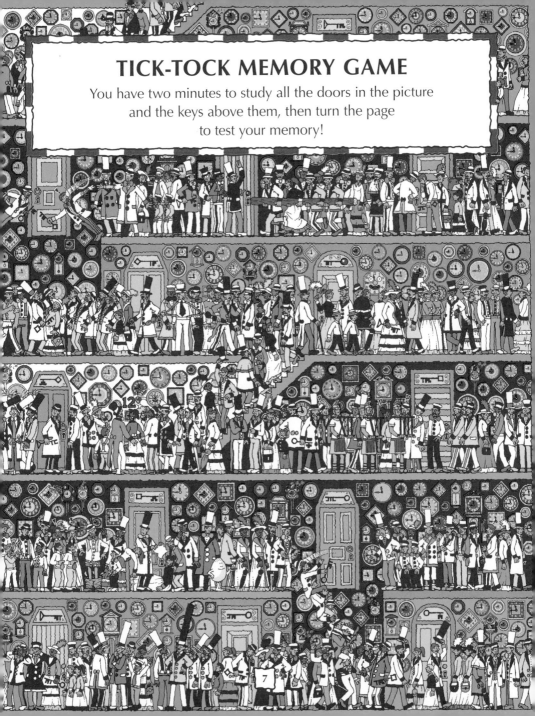

TICK-TOCK MEMORY GAME

You have two minutes to study all the doors in the picture
and the keys above them, then turn the page
to test your memory!

TICK-TOCK MEMORY GAME

Can you remember which key goes above which door?
Draw a line from each key to the door it opens.

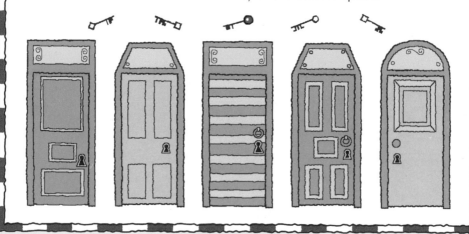

THROUGH THE KEYHOLE GAME

Take your time to peek through these keyholes.
Then turn back the page and find each section in the scene.

PYRAMID PUZZLE

Search for the words at the bottom of this page in the pyramid puzzle.
The words go up, down, forwards and backwards –
just like an Egyptian dance!

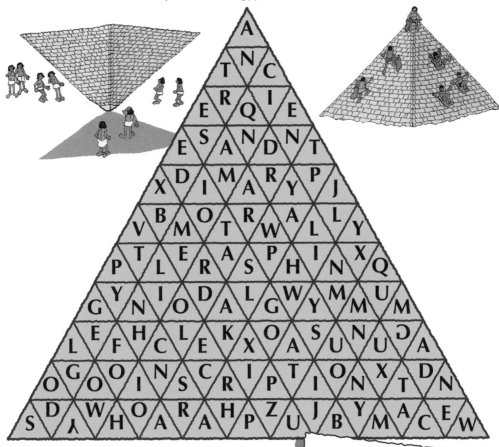

CAT • PYRAMID • SUN • ANCIENT
DESERT • WALLY • GODS • SAND
MUMMY • NILE • GOAT • PHARAOH
INSCRIPTION • TOMB • SPHINX • EGYPT

MORE THINGS TO FIND

☐ A back-to-front letter

☐ An upside-down letter

☐ The names of two of Wally's friends (from page 2)

WILD AND WACKY W'S

Can you fit all the W words in the puzzle? One of the words has *wandered* backwards, and another doesn't begin with W but is *all over*.

WAHOO

WAVE

WHOOPEE

WHOOSH

WONDER

EVERYWHERE

WEB

WHIZZ

WITTY

WILD

WAVE

WIG

WOW

WISE

REDNAW

WACKY

MORE THINGS TO DO

How quickly can you say this tongue-twister? Wally wishes Wenda would wear a waterproof watch!

BALLOON BEDLAM

What a terrific tangle! Follow the strings to find out
which balloons Wally and his friends are holding.

MORE THINGS TO DO

Look at the patterns
in the border to find
a sequence that
matches the order of
the patterns on the
balloons. Then colour
in the empty balloon.

STARS AND STRIPES

Which stripy path leads from Wally's seal to the golden star?
You better hurry – there are multiple Wallies trying to reach it!

MORE THINGS TO FIND
- [ ] A stripy walking stick
- [ ] A hat with a blue bobble

FUNNY FACE FLAGS

What a frenzied flurry of fierce and funny flags! Can you find these eleven foolish faces in the scene below?

MORE THINGS TO FIND

☐ Two snakes

☐ A game of noughts and crosses

☐ Ten milk bottles

13

TERRIFIC TRAVELS!

Study the pictures of the extraordinary places Wally has visited and fill in the answers to each question below.

How many red birds?

_____

How many custard pies have been thrown?

_____

How many sunglasses?

_____

How many green hoods?

_____

How many yellow fish?

_____

How many hats with feathers?

_____

How many moustaches?

_____

MORE THINGS TO FIND

☐ Wally's spare pair of glasses

☐ A red-and-yellow feather

☐ Odlaw in a Wally hat

PHEW! WHAT A WILD RIDE THAT WAS. YOU'RE A REAL BRAIN BOX IF YOU BEAT THOSE BEFUDDLING FLIGHTS OF FANCY! BUT DON'T TAKE OFF YOUR THINKING CAPS YET – WE'VE STILL GOT A LONG WAY TO GO ON OUR JOURNEY ... CARRY ON, WALLY-WATCHERS!

Can you find where these pictures come from in Wally's chapter? But beware, there is one picture from elsewhere in the book!

WALLY'S CHECKLIST

Wait, there's more! Look back over Wally's journey and find...

- ☐ A clown with a cone-shaped head
- ☐ A Roman clock
- ☐ Three people talking on walkie-talkies
- ☐ A soldier with a white beard
- ☐ Two clocks with smiling faces
- ☐ Two clowns sharing a hat
- ☐ An egg timer
- ☐ A set of tea-shirts
- ☐ A cake with nine candles
- ☐ A dog wearing sunglasses
- ☐ People sliding on mats

ONE LAST THING...

Can you find Wally's key hidden somewhere in this section? Keep your eyes peeled – there are some trick keys out there! 🔑

BOW - WOW!

RUFF RUFF! WOOF HERE! ARE YOU READY FOR SOME TAIL-WAGGINGLY GOOD GAMES? MY POOCH PALS AND I HAVE BEEN REALLY PUZZLING OVER THE CHALLENGES AHEAD, AND WE'RE HOPING YOU CAN HELP US OUT. THERE ARE PLENTY OF ANSWERS FOR YOU TO SNIFF OUT, SO TAKE THE LEAD AND FOLLOW ME THROUGH THESE CRAZY CANINE CONUNDRUMS. GOOD LUCK!

BARE BONES BRAIN BUSTER

Take your time to study this scene very closely.
Then turn the page to test your memory.

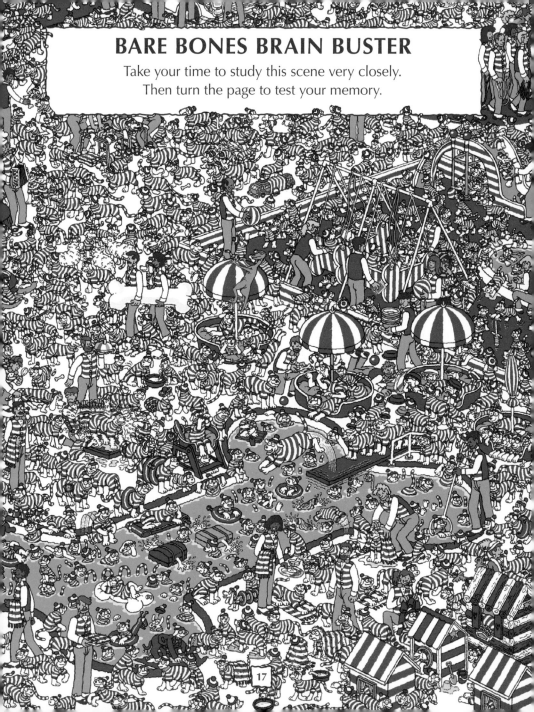

BARE BONES BRAIN BUSTER

Here goes! How many of these questions can you answer from memory? (It's also fun to guess!) Then turn back the page to see how you did.

1. Which of Wally's friends is visiting?
- ☐ Wenda
- ☐ Wizard Whitebeard
- ☐ Odlaw

2. What colour are the staff's bow ties?
- ☐ Red
- ☐ Blue
- ☐ White

3. How many parasols are there?
- ☐ Three
- ☐ Four
- ☐ Five

4. What long, white thing are two waiters carrying?
- ☐ A bone
- ☐ A lead
- ☐ A pogo-stick

5. What instrument is Woof's waiter playing?
- ☐ Piano
- ☐ Accordion
- ☐ Guitar

6. What equipment can be found in the playground?
- ☐ Swings and a roundabout
- ☐ A seesaw and a slide
- ☐ Swings and a slide

EXTRA BONE-OCULAR EYE-BOGGLER

Study these close-ups carefully then turn back the page to find them in the scene.

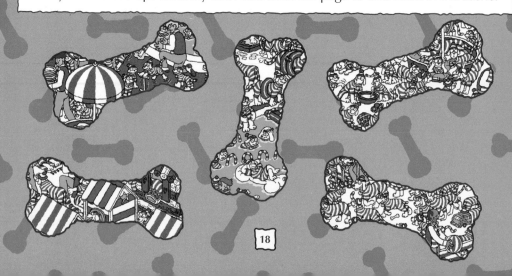

WAG TAIL WAY OUT

Find a way through the maze of Woof tails. Start at the square
with the red tail and use the guide below to help
you reach the square with the white tail.

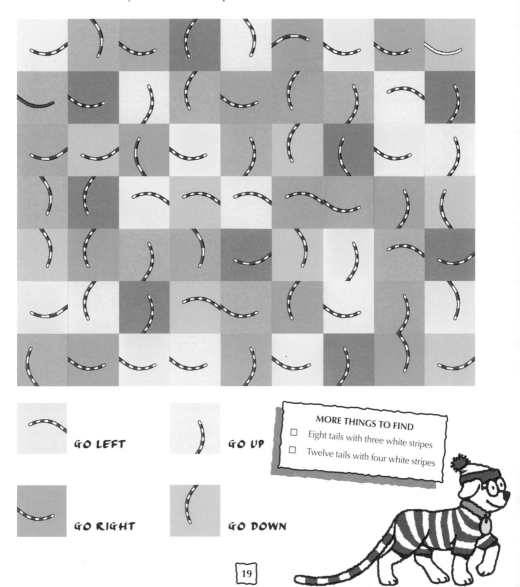

GO LEFT

GO UP

GO RIGHT

GO DOWN

MORE THINGS TO FIND

☐ Eight tails with three white stripes

☐ Twelve tails with four white stripes

WHO'S WHO?

What a mix-up! Unscramble the anagrams to fill in the boxes below.
Then draw a line to match the pictures to your answers.

OWOF	
GIMNCIAA	
YALWL	
ALYWL AWCTERH	
VEMCANA	
IPARET	
RIOSNDAU	
CTAROAB	
IGHNKT	
GIKINV	

MORE THINGS TO DO
Write an anagram of your name in the empty space!

WOOF'S WORD WHEEL

Use the clues to help you find five words using three or more letters in the word wheel. Each answer must contain the letter O only once.

CLUES

1. It's as hard as rock
2. Woof's favourite thing
3. Used to sniff
4. Heads, shoulders, knees and...
5. Woof is one of these

2.

3.

4.

1.

5.

MORE THINGS TO DO
See how many other words you can make using the word wheel.

TRUTH OR TAILS?

Test your knowledge of Woof's ancient four-legged friends and work out which statements are true and which are false.

1. The word dinosaur means 'terrible lizard'.

2. A dinosaur scientist is called a dinotologist.

3. Dinosaurs laid eggs.

4. This anagram spells a dinosaur's name: RETTSRIPOCA

5. A Tyrannosaurus' bite was roughly three times stronger than that of a lion.

6. The Ankylosaurus had a club tail.

7. The dinosaur with the longest name is called a Micropachycephalosaurus.

8. A Pterodactyl had three wings.

9. A Brachiosaurus had a very short neck.

10. The dinosaurs lived until 65 thousand years ago.

Use the Internet or an encyclopaedia to help you, and look up more fun facts about dinosaurs.

DID YOU KNOW?

There was a dinosaur similar to a dog! It is called Cynognathus (sy-nog-nay-thus) and was a hairy mammal-like animal with dog-like teeth. Woof claims that his great-great-great grandfather was one (calculated in dog years, of course)!

ONE MORE THING

What is the name of the dinosaur whose skeleton is in this picture? *Clue: it begins with the letter 'S'.*

DOG'S DINNER

Scribble out all the W's to decode Woof's message
and write the answer in the spaces below each line.
A double W means a break between words.

W O W N W W Y W O W U W R W W B W A W R W K W S ,

W W G W E W T W W S W E W T , W W G W O ! W W M W Y W W P W A W L W S

W W A W N W D W W I W W A W R W E W W W C W H W W A W S W I W N W G

W W O W U W R W W F W A W V W O W U W R W I W T W E

W W T W H W I W N W G W S : W W S W A W U W S W A W G W E W S ,

W W B W O W N W E W S W W A W N W D W W C W A W W T W S !

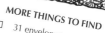

MORE THINGS TO FIND

☐ 31 envelopes

☐ A dog that is not wearing a collar

☐ Two blue dog bowls

BURIED BONES

Woof has been busy burying bones! Can you fill in
the grid coordinates for the items at the bottom of
the page that mark where he has hidden them?

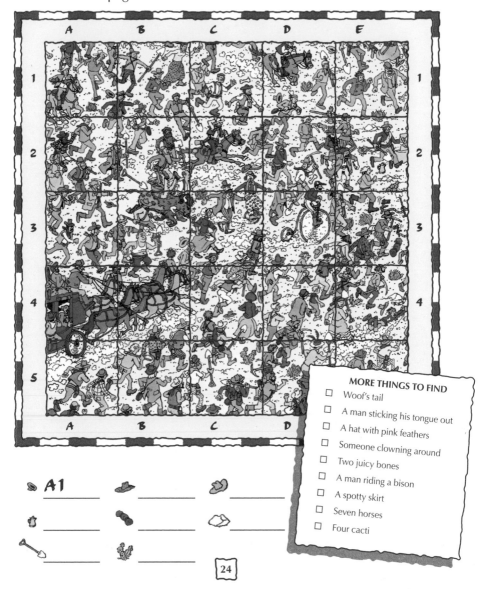

MORE THINGS TO FIND

- [ ] Woof's tail
- [ ] A man sticking his tongue out
- [ ] A hat with pink feathers
- [ ] Someone clowning around
- [ ] Two juicy bones
- [ ] A man riding a bison
- [ ] A spotty skirt
- [ ] Seven horses
- [ ] Four cacti

A1 _____

RUFF RUFF! YOU'RE CERTAINLY NO BONEHEAD! THANKS FOR HELPING ME AND MY POOCH PALS PICK APART THESE PUZZLES. WE LIKE TO KEEP YOU ON YOUR PAWS, SO KEEP GOING FOR MORE FUN AND GAMES!

PLUS THERE'S MORE PUPPY PUZZLES BELOW!

Can you spot these pictures somewhere in Woof's chapter? But hold your horses, one picture is from a different place entirely!

WOOF'S CHECKLIST

Pad back through Woof's wonderful wanders and find…

- ☐ Seven red dog bowls
- ☐ A watch dog
- ☐ A penny farthing
- ☐ A sandcastle
- ☐ A falling tree
- ☐ Sherlock Woof
- ☐ A man being poked by a spear
- ☐ A cat dressed as Woof
- ☐ A rubber duck
- ☐ A woman wearing a fur coat
- ☐ A bluebird wearing a bobble hat

ONE LAST THING…

Can you find Woof's bone in this section? Don't be fooled by any fake bones!

HI THERE, SHARP-EYED THRILL SEEKERS!

ARE YOU READY FOR THE NEXT ROUND OF WILD WORDS, SUPER SEARCHES AND BRILLIANT BRAIN GAMES? IT'S BEEN A CRAZY JOURNEY SO FAR, BUT NOW IS YOUR CHANCE TO TAKE ON SOME REAL CHALLENGES. THERE'S LOTS OF CAMERA CHAOS AND MUSICAL MAYHEM ON THE PAGES AHEAD – SO STAY SHARP!

GOOD LUCK, ADVENTURERS!

SNAPPY SINGING!

These stamping feet are creating cracks everywhere in this spectacular singing scene. Can you find the seven broken things from the list below?

BROKEN THINGS TO FIND
- [ ] A smashed mirror
- [ ] Woof's snapped bone
- [ ] A bent umbrella
- [ ] A split stage
- [ ] A broken walking stick
- [ ] A ladder with a broken rung
- [ ] Wenda's broken spectacles

A COLOURFUL TUNE

Can you find these sets of musical notes inside the puzzle?
The answers run across, down and diagonally.

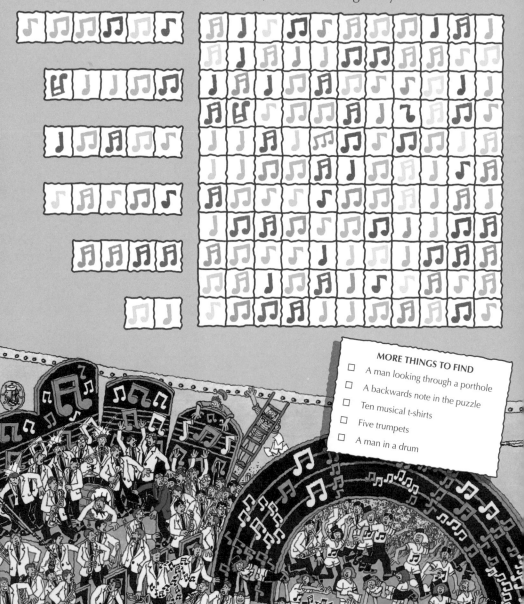

MORE THINGS TO FIND

☐ A man looking through a porthole
☐ A backwards note in the puzzle
☐ Ten musical t-shirts
☐ Five trumpets
☐ A man in a drum

BUSY BANDSTAND

What a musical muddle! Look at the clapper board and match up the instruments with the pieces needed to play.

DRUM
CLARINET
GUITAR
TROMBONE
VIOLIN
TRIANGLE
PIANO

MOUTHPIECE
BOW
KEYS
ROD
PICK
REED
STICKS

MORE THINGS TO DO
Find animal costumes in the scene beginning with B, C, P and R.

Sing your favourite song!

UNDER THE SPOTLIGHT

Lights, camera, action! Can you spot ten differences between these two musical scenes?

MORE THINGS TO DO

Create your own checklist of things to find in the scenes.

- ☐ ....
- ☐ ....
- ☐ ....
- ☐ ....
- ☐ ....

LOST LUGGAGE

Spot Wenda's lost luggage in these photographs.
Can you find one bag with a red-and-white striped luggage label,
two bags with white labels and two bags with blue labels?

MORE THINGS TO FIND
- [ ] A bag with a red luggage label
- [ ] A woman wearing yellow shoes
- [ ] A barrel
- [ ] Seven yellow luggage labels

CAKE-TASTROPHE!

Help Wenda figure out all the ingredients for this cake recipe by scribbling out the letters in grey that spell 'Wenda' in every word.

WSEUGNADRA

WBEUNTTDEAR

EWGENGDAS

SWELF ERAISNINDG FLOAUR

VWANEILLNA EDSSEANCE

BWAEKING NPODWDAER

MORE THINGS TO FIND

☐ A gingerbread person

☐ Wenda's cake with three red layers

☐ A double-ended wooden spoon

32

CAMERA CLOSE-UPS

Whoops, Wenda's camera is broken! Can you work out who she has accidentally zoomed into? Some people appear more than once.

1.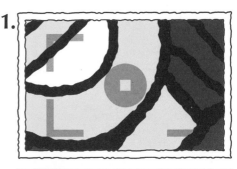

2.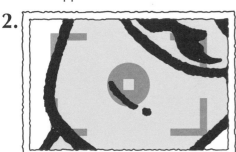

3.

4.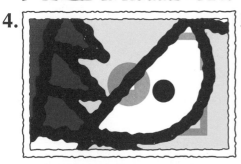

5.

6.

7.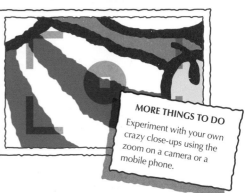

MORE THINGS TO DO
Experiment with your own crazy close-ups using the zoom on a camera or a mobile phone.

MUSICAL FRAME FUN

Wenda has framed her favourite musical photographs. Can you find a picture that doesn't contain a musical note, and one frame with Wenda's face in the border?

MORE THINGS TO FIND

- ☐ Twelve violins
- ☐ A large bow tie
- ☐ A guitar
- ☐ Three tubas
- ☐ A one-eyed man

DANCING SILHOUETTES

Wenda has sent you a postcard from the after-show party.
Match the silhouettes with her funky-stepping friends on the dance floor.

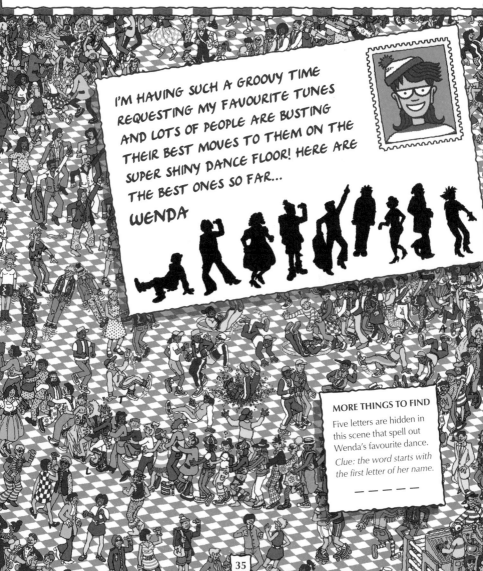

I'M HAVING SUCH A GROOVY TIME REQUESTING MY FAVOURITE TUNES AND LOTS OF PEOPLE ARE BUSTING THEIR BEST MOVES TO THEM ON THE SUPER SHINY DANCE FLOOR! HERE ARE THE BEST ONES SO FAR...

WENDA

MORE THINGS TO FIND

Five letters are hidden in this scene that spell out Wenda's favourite dance.

Clue: the word starts with the first letter of her name.

_ _ _ _ _

WOBBLY WORD LADDERS

Hang on! Can you fill in the missing words in these ladders?
Start at the top and work your way down by changing one letter
at a time, but keeping the rest of the letters in the same order.

HAT

_ _ _

_ _ _

KEY

MALT

_ _ _ _

_ _ _ _

_ _ _ _

GAME

MORE THINGS TO FIND
☐ A hat with a red bobble
☐ A parrot
☐ Someone sticking out their tongue

WOW! WHAT A SAVVY SEARCHER YOU ARE! DID YOU FIND IT TOUGH TACKLING ALL THOSE SCRAMBLED SCENES AND WACKY WORDS? I HOPE IT WASN'T TOO TRICKY – THERE ARE STILL SOME MIND-BOGGLERS FOR YOU TO BATTLE WITH... KEEP GOING, BRAIN BOXES!

Enjoy searching for these pictures in Wenda's chapter. Watch that you don't spend too long looking for one of them, because it's from a different section!

WENDA'S CHECKLIST

Flick back through Wenda's extravaganza and find...

- ☐ Two Wendas wearing blue shoes
- ☐ A man with his head stuck in a tap
- ☐ A ball gown
- ☐ Frankenstein's monster
- ☐ Kettle drums
- ☐ A black-and-yellow luggage label
- ☐ Wizard Brownbeard
- ☐ A mouth organ
- ☐ An apple with a pie
- ☐ A disc jockey
- ☐ A sole singer

ONE LAST THING...

Did you spot Wenda's camera? Only this one is picture-perfect ... the others are fake, so be on the lookout!

WORD CASTLE

Find the words at the bottom of this page in the three-letter bricks of this castle. A word can read across more than one brick.

R	O	F			A	Q	U	E	E	N			A	X	E
M	X	A			J	O	P	W	W	O			W	G	R
L	W	A	D	R	A	W	B	R	I	D	G	E	H	L	D	R	A
O	A	R	M	O	U	R	E	K	R	C	A	T	A	P	U	L	T
N	T	P	C	A	S	T	L	E	L	Q	P	U	F	M	P	X	E
W	Q	L	E	U	H	E	L	M	E	T	A	B	A	T	T	L	E
M	O	A	T	H	Y	K	W	S	E	M	I	U	L	E	I	A	F
D	G	E	M	I	L	A	I	N	S	I	S	W	O	R	D	W	R
A	R	R	O	W	H	R	E	E	A	K	L	K	C	E	T	L	H
H	F	M	A	R	A	W	N	P	M	T	L	H	F	L	A	G	T
W	K	I	N	G	O	H	Y	O	E	A	B	O	S	P	P	C	G

MORE THINGS TO DO

Work out the two magic words that can open the castle drawbridge. Then find it hidden in the word castle!

Clue: the letters go up, across and down.

O _ _ _ / _ _ S _ _ E

WORDS TO FIND

ARMOUR

SWORD

MOAT

ARROW

CASTLE

DRAWBRIDGE

CATAPULT

KING

QUEEN

HELMET

AXE

BATTLE

MIX-UP MADNESS

What a muddle! Match the top halves of these characters
to the correct bottom halves.

MORE THINGS TO DO
- Draw your own fantasy characters in the two blank boxes!
- Give some of the mixed-up characters combination names, like "Vikingator" (viking + gladiator)!

GIANT GAME

Start on the board game square next to each player's picture.
Then follow their footstep guide to work out who picks up the scroll.

MORE THINGS TO FIND

☐ Nine men wearing helmets

☐ Someone wearing blue-and-yellow tights

☐ Four pitchforks

SOMETHING FISHY

Match up the sets of three identically coloured fish. One fish is not part of a set, so have a splish-splashing time finding out which one!

MORE THINGS TO FIND

- [ ] A smiling fish
- [ ] An angry fish
- [ ] A fish with closed eyes

42

TELEPORTATION TANGLE

Beam me up! What a tangle! Follow the teleportation rays to find out who's travelling where.

MORE THINGS TO DO
How many books is Wally holding? What do you think they're about?

SHIELDS AND STAVES

En garde, eyes at the ready! Find two pictures that are the same.

MORE THINGS TO FIND
- [ ] Four blue shields
- [ ] Eight green hats
- [ ] A carved red staff
- [ ] A man with stars above his head

GENIE-OUS!

Draw in the missing symbols to release the genie from its lamp! All nine symbols must appear once in each box, but never in the same row.

MORE THINGS TO DO

If you were granted three wishes, what would they be?

1. ....

2. ....

3. ....

DOUBLE VISION

All is not what it seems with these magic monks and red-cloaked ghouls.
Spot six differences between these two scenes.

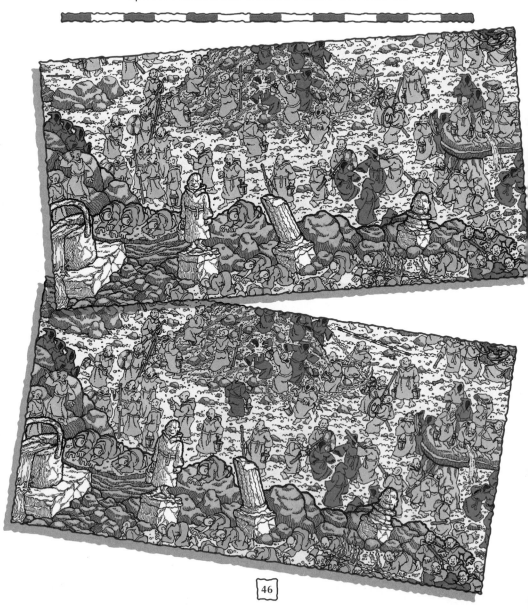

WHICH WITCH IS WHICH?

Read the witchy riddles and match them to the pictures.

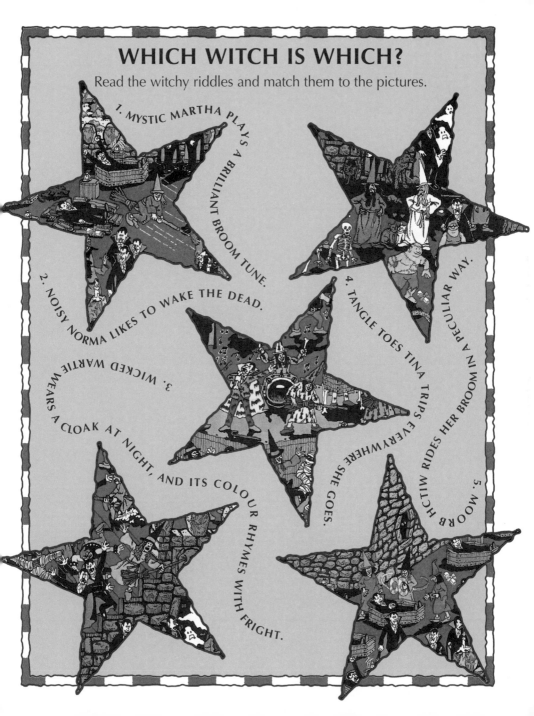

1. MYSTIC MARTHA PLAYS A BRILLIANT BROOM TUNE.

2. NOISY NORMA LIKES TO WAKE THE DEAD.

3. WICKED WARTIE WEARS A CLOAK AT NIGHT, AND ITS COLOUR RHYMES WITH FRIGHT.

4. TANGLE TOES TINA TRIPS EVERYWHERE SHE GOES.

5. MOORB HCTIW RIDES HER BROOM IN A PECULIAR WAY.

WISE CRACKS

Wizard Whitebeard has cast a happy spell!
This scroll is inscribed with lots of jokes.
Which one makes you laugh the most?

WHAT'S SO SPECIAL ABOUT THE
WAY WIZARDS SERVE THEIR TEA?

THEY GIVE YOU BISCUITS
ON A FLYING SORCERER!

MORE THINGS TO DO
Make up your own
joke and write it in the
space on the scroll!

HOW MANY WIZARDS DOES IT TAKE
TO CAST A SPELL OF INVISIBILITY?

I DON'T KNOW, I CAN'T SEE THEM!

HOW CAN YOU DESCRIBE
A WIZARD'S BOOK?

SPELL-BINDING!

WHY CAN'T WIZARDS
CLEAN FLOORS?

BECAUSE THE WITCHES
STOLE THEIR BROOMS!

WHAT DID THE MAGICIAN DO
WHEN HE WAS VERY ANGRY?

HE PULLED HIS HARE OUT!

....

....

....

BLESS MY BEARD, YOU HAVE A TRULY MAGICAL MIND! CONGRATULATIONS ON WORKING THROUGH MY SILLY SORCERY. YOU'RE NEARLY AT THE END OF THIS TRICKSY PATH OF PUZZLES AND PANDEMONIUM, BUT NOT YET! THERE ARE STILL PLENTY OF TESTS ON THIS QUIZZICAL QUEST. I WISH YOU THE VERY BEST OF LUCK...

Can you spot these scenes from Wizard Whitebeard's section? But riddle me this – one of them comes from somewhere else in the book!

WIZARD WHITEBEARD'S SCROLL CHECKLIST

Cast your eyes over Wizard Whitebeard's quest and find...

☐ Wizard Whitebeard in a boat
☐ A sea lion
☐ A windmill
☐ Four jumping fish
☐ A gargoyle breathing fire
☐ Three genies
☐ A man who has gone through a shield
☐ A wishing well
☐ A skeleton
☐ A minstrel with a terrible singing voice
☐ Two cats in love

ONE LAST THING...

Have you spotted Wizard Whitebeard's scroll somewhere in this section? Only the scroll with the red bow contains the right magic spell...

49

TOP FIENDS

Meet Odlaw's most ferocious team of fiends. Look at the pictures on the cards and match them to the correct description.

Name: Hungry Growler

Lives: Swamps

Favourite Food: Everything and anything

Speed: Lumbering

Courage: 10

Spy Ability: 2

Fear Factor: 8

Special Skill: Roaring and emitting foul smells

Name: Heave Ho Henry

Lives: Dungeons

Favourite Food: Nuts and bolts

Speed: Slow when rusty

Courage: 4

Spy Ability: 9

Fear Factor: 10

Special Skill: Sneaking up on people

Name: Captain Cutlass

Lives: The Black Skull Ship

Favourite Food: Dried meats

Speed: Peg-leg slow

Courage: 9

Spy Ability: 6

Fear Factor: 6

Special Skill: Pillaging

Name: Warty Gretel

Lives: The Witch's Castle

Favourite Food: Bats' tails, frogs' legs, eyes of a newt

Speed: Fast on a broom

Courage: 4

Spy Ability: 10

Fear Factor: 6

Special Skill: Potions and curses

MORE THINGS TO DO

* Who ranks the highest for their spying skills?
* Who is the most courageous?
* Who is the most terrifying?

SUPER SNEAKY SEA-GAZING GAME

Odlaw loves to look out at sea with his pirate friends. Study the scene very closely and spot everything noted in the ship's logbook below.

☐ Three men wearing skull and crossbones t-shirts

☐ Two hats with green feathers

☐ Three men with yellow beards

☐ Five men wearing red-and-white stripy trousers

☐ Three men wearing yellow bandanas with black spots

☐ Five flying cutlasses

SUPER SNEAKY SEA-GAZING GAME

How closely did you study Odlaw's pirate scene? Look through these binocular views and find each section on the previous page.

RIDDLING RIDDLES AND TWISTY TONGUE TWISTERS

How many times can you repeat
Black and yellow stripes –
Yellow and black stripes.
without getting tongue-tied?

Can you decode this riddle
to find out who is keeping Odlaw
company aboard ship?
My hands hang low
But my tail swings high,
See if you can spot me
Dangling in the sky.

Repeat this sentence
five times and see how
tangled your tongue gets!
Pirate Plunderers
Seek Scallywag
Scupperers.

What am I?
I have eight legs and two big eyes,
but don't look for me in the skies.

MONOCHROME MONSTERS

Finish this monstrous tower
scene with your wackiest colours!

MORE THINGS TO FIND

☐ Seven spotty dragons

☐ Nine ladders

☐ A dragon flying upside down

☐ A sailor in stripy clothes

☐ A dragon wearing flying goggles

55

SNAKING WORDS

Read the clues and work out the answers by joining up the letters inside each frame without taking your pen off the paper!

1. Clue: A sea-travelling invader

N I
G K
V I

2. Clue: A sword-swishing soldier

E T E
K M E
S U R

3. Clue: A skeletal symbol used by pirates

K S S E B S
U A N N O S
L L D C R O

MORE THINGS TO FIND

☐ Nine yellow-headed birds

☐ Three Draculas

☐ A flying witch

PIRATEY PUZZLE

Ahoy there! Fill in the answers next to these questions to reveal a word going downwards that is Odlaw's favourite part of a piratey disguise!

The... seas (*clue: number of days in a week*)

Observing in secret

The rear part of a ship

Person in charge of the ship and its crew

Odlaw's treasure-hunting shipmates

Message in a...

Heavy weight on rope keeping a ship in one place

Pieces of... (*clue: a number between seven and nine*)

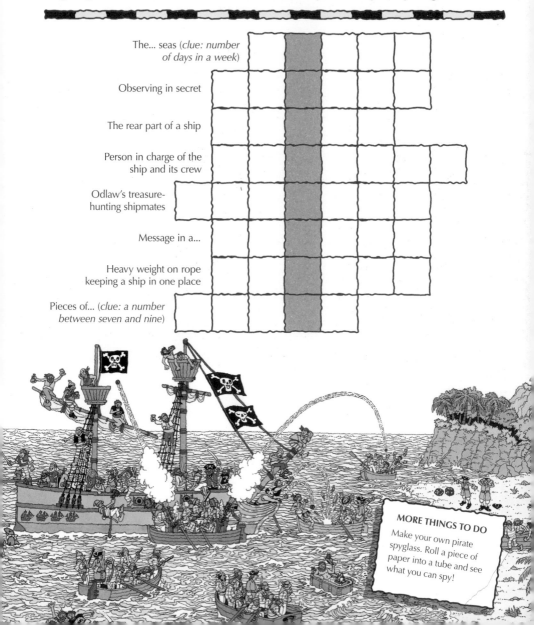

MORE THINGS TO DO

Make your own pirate spyglass. Roll a piece of paper into a tube and see what you can spy!

SLIPPERY SEARCH

Using your finger, trace a path through the tunnels to help Odlaw escape and pick up his slithery black-and-yellow striped companion on the way.

WELL, WELL, WELL ... THIS IS A SURPRISE. CONGRATULATIONS, YOU'RE ALMOST AS CUNNING AS I AM. MAYBE NEXT TIME YOU CAN JOIN ON MY QUEST TO FOIL WALLY ... BUT FOR NOW, THERE ARE STILL SOME THINGS FOR YOU TO FIND! DID YOU REALLY THINK IT WAS GOING TO BE THAT EASY? GOOD LUCK, I SUPPOSE...

Can you spot where these pictures come from in Odlaw's chapter? Be careful, one is from somewhere else in the book!

ODLAW'S CHECKLIST

Wait, there's more! Look back through the pictures and find...

- ☐ Three yellow-and-black stripy top hats
- ☐ A love bird
- ☐ A winking skull and crossbones
- ☐ A seagull captain
- ☐ A tunnel traffic controller
- ☐ A man in a bath boat
- ☐ A sleeping dragon
- ☐ A woman in a red beret
- ☐ A monkey on a mast
- ☐ A monster stealing a hat
- ☐ A lightweight boxer

ONE LAST THING...

Can you spot Odlaw's binoculars in this section? Only search for them if you dare...

ANSWERS

P. 5 TRAVEL ESSENTIALS
MORE THINGS TO DO

cirgan rac = racing car; dgrna iapno = grand piano; ckhneti snki = kitchen sink

P. 9 PYRAMID PUZZLE

P. 10 WILD AND WACKY W'S

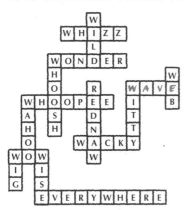

P. 11 BALLOON BEDLAM

MORE THINGS TO DO
The missing pattern is the spotty balloon.

P. 12 STARS AND STRIPES
The path marked in yellow leads to Wally's golden star.

P. 14 TERRIFIC TRAVELS!
4 red birds; 7 custard pies; 5 pairs of sunglasses; 9 green hoods; 7 yellow fish; 9 hats with feathers; 8 moustaches

P. 18 BARE BONES BRAIN BUSTER

1. Odlaw; 2. blue; 3. three; 4. a bone;
5. accordion; 6. swings and a slide

P. 19 WAG TAIL WAY OUT

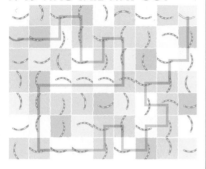

P. 20 WHO'S WHO?

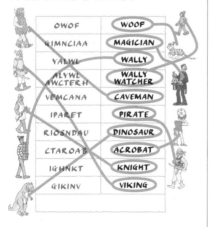

OWOF	WOOF
GIMNCIAA	MAGICIAN
YALWL	WALLY
ALYWL WCTERH	WALLY WATCHER
VEMCANA	CAVEMAN
IPARET	PIRATE
RIOSNDAU	DINOSAUR
CTAROAB	ACROBAT
IGHNKT	KNIGHT
GIKINV	VIKING

P. 21 WOOF'S WORD WHEEL

1. stone; 2. bone; 3. nose; 4. toes; 5. dog

P. 22 TRUTH OR TAILS?

1. True; 2. False: a dinosaur scientist
is called a palaeontologist; 3. True;
4. True: TRICERATOPS; 5. True;
6. True; 7. True; 8. False: it had two
wings; 9. False: it had a very long neck;
10. False: dinosaurs actually lived until
65 million years ago – wow!

ONE MORE THING
Stegosaurus

P. 23 DOG'S DINNER

ON YOUR BARKS, GET SET, GO! MY PALS
AND I ARE CHASING OUR FAVOURITE
THINGS: SAUSAGES, BONES AND CATS!

P. 28 A COLOURFUL TUNE

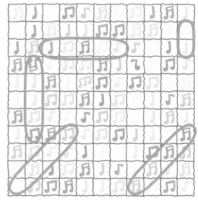

P. 29 BUSY BANDSTAND

drum – sticks; clarinet – reed;
guitar – pick; trombone – mouthpiece;
violin – bow; triangle – rod; piano – keys

P. 32 CAKE-TASTROPHE!

sugar; butter; eggs; self raising flour; vanilla essence; baking powder

P. 33 CAMERA CLOSE-UPS

1. Wenda; 2. Odlaw; 3. Wally; 4. Wenda;
5. Wizard Whitebeard; 6. Wally; 7. Woof

P. 35 DANCING SILHOUETTES

MORE THINGS TO FIND

Wenda's favourite dance is the waltz.

P. 36 WOBBLY WORD LADDERS

Here is one possible solution:
HAT, HAY, HEY, KEY
MALT, SALT, SALE, SAME, GAME

P. 39 WORD CASTLE

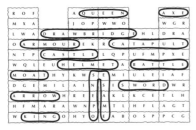

MORE THINGS TO DO

The two magic words are 'Open Sesame'.

P. 40 MIX-UP MADNESS

P. 41 GIANT GAME

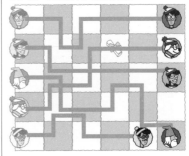

P. 42 SOMETHING FISHY

P. 43 TELEPORTATION TANGLE

P. 44 SHIELDS AND STAVES

P. 45 GENIE-OUS!

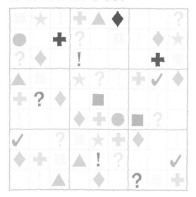

P. 47 WHICH WITCH IS WHICH?

P. 52 TOP FIENDS

Warty Gretel

Heave Ho Henry

Captain Cutlass

Hungry Growler

P. 54 RIDDLING RIDDLES AND TWISTY TONGUE TWISTERS

My hands hang low
But my tail swings high…
A: A monkey
I have eight legs and two big eyes…
A: An octopus

P. 56 SNAKING WORDS

1. viking; 2. musketeer; 3. skull and crossbones

P. 57 PIRATEY PUZZLE

```
    S E V E N
  S P Y I N G
  S T E R N
  C A P T A I N
P I R A T E S
B O T T L E
A N C H O R
E I G H T
```

P. 58 SLIPPERY SEARCH

First published 2012 by Walker Books Ltd, 87 Vauxhall Walk, London SE11 5HJ as *The Search For The Lost Things* • This edition published 2018 • 2 4 6 8 10 9 7 5 3 1 • © 1987–2018 Martin Handford • The right of Martin Handford to be identified as author/illustrator of this work has been asserted by him in accordance with the Copyright, Designs and Patents Act 1988 • This book has been typeset in Wallyfont and Optima • Printed in China • All rights reserved. • British Library Cataloguing in Publication Data: a catalogue record for this book is available from the British Library • ISBN 978-1-4063-8118-4 • www.walker.co.uk

ONE *VERY* LAST THING...

The fun and games aren't over!
Can you find a puzzle piece
and a pair of dice hidden
somewhere in this book?
Happy hunting!